Angels

C000150352

& Gods

Everything in Heaven and

Hell is not always as it

seems

Contents

The Nature of Love (Anywhere and Everywhere)

24 Hours

Once upon a time...many, many years ago...*woah! Hold on! Let's just drop the transparent 'Anywhere as Planet Earth' metaphor and set this tale exactly where it actually takes place – your own world, right here and right now...*

One particular day, some time around now, if you like, God (by chance rather design) looked down upon the Earth. This was something He, in his Infinite Wisdom, rarely did. You see, God, by nature, is a tinkerer with a very short attention span and, having created Earth some eons past he had moved on to other things – new planets, new challenges. The fact that Earth was also a failed experiment (that whole Humans and 'free will' thing...well, what a disaster...less said, soonest mended!) that had been at the heart of the rupture between God and his beloved old friend, The Devil, meant that God was even less likely to bother with Earth than any of the other myriad planets he'd created.

But...seeing as planet Earth had come into his view, God decided, reluctantly, that he'd better have a quick look at what was going on, take some notes and do some Supreme Being 'making judgements' type stuff as per the Universe had empowered and mandated him to do.

And so God looked at Earth. And he wished he hadn't.

In England, a prominent politician and a famous celebrity, in a large and richly furnished room in an extremely expensive London property, rape a twelve year old girl. After they've raped her, they murder her...they do this because they enjoy it and because they can get away with it.

In America, a homeless man settles down to try and sleep behind a dumpster, situated down a dank and dark, piss-reeking New York alleyway; four bankers – drunk on expensive champagne and their own arrogance, have followed him to his insecure, uncomfortable place of rest. They are playing 'hunt the bum'. With laughs and whoops, they kick and stamp the homeless man to death.

In Yemen, 29 school children are blown to pieces by a bomb dropped from a fighter jet flying high above...the children are, apparently, a legitimate military target.

In Brazil, a death squad, sent by a newly elected fascist government (elected with the help and support of Wall Street bankers), kidnaps and murders 12 student activists.

In Spain, a drunken, inadequate man beats his wife to death because she's annoyed him (she's such a nag..) and because she's his property, after all.

In Libya, once a rich nation but destroyed by the greed, avarice and evil of wicked and wealthy old men who dream only of profit and power (you know, the ones who own our politicians...read the next tale), a slave market is trading; women and children fetch the best price – they'll make good money for their new owners as prostitutes and as the unwitting stars of snuff movies; healthy young men are also prized, they'll be killed and their organs harvested and sold to those who are old and sick but wealthy and amoral.

In Nigeria, a two year old child is dying slowly and horribly of starvation whilst, at the same time, a wealthy woman and her husband enters an upmarket store in a fashionable Paris street. She spends $250,000 on a new handbag and he even more on a new watch.

On and on and on it goes, minute after minute, hour after hour...a depressing, sickening litany of murder and evil and injustice and cruelty and tragedy and sadness and prejudice and torture and rape and degradation and stupidity and violence and ignorance.

And God, repulsed and disgusted by all he had seen, thought to himself...

'Oh...what have I done? The Devil was always my Wiser Half...had I but listened to his advice instead of casting him out then I would never even have made this Earth and these horrible humans with their dangerous free will! Maybe now is the time to admit that this Earth and these Humans are, indeed, a failed experiment, a planet and a species inhabited by boundless evil that should be destroyed.'

But then, one hundred miles off the coast of south eastern Spain, a small boat, dangerously overloaded with desperate refugees, men, women and children, fleeing yet another land destroyed and broken by a war fought for no other reason than to make obscene and obscenely rich old men even more obscenely rich, capsizes in rough seas. There are fifty one refugees packed into the boat..most of them are sucked down to their deaths beneath the hungry, cold water with the sinking vessel. Ten minutes later only five people remain alive, bobbing up and down on sharp, serrated waves. Twenty minutes later only three people remain alive, five minutes after that, only two; a young mother and her six month old baby boy.

As she cradles the child in her arms, Nimah (let's dignify this poor young woman with a name for we are, after all, to bare witness to her death) tries pointlessly to shield her infant son from the cold and hostile sea (the boy's name is, was, Malik – what would he have been, what would he have done had he been allowed to grow up rather than been sacrificed for the benefit of the already bulging wallets of the psychopathic elite who rules us?).

The child cries. He's desperately cold and instinctively feels his mothers fear.

Nimah tries hard, so very, very hard, to keep herself and her child afloat, in the hope that help may come. But at some point, Nimah realises that hope of rescue is in vain and she's so tired and so cold...as hope slides away so does her strength....slowly she slips beneath the sea and her last act on this Earth is to put every last ounce of energy she has into lifting Malik up above her head to delay his descent into the cold and hungry ocean; to give him as many last few seconds of this precious gift of life that she possibly can. Finally, as Malik's little head is also embraced by the sea, Nimah summons from somewhere (I would say 'God knows where' but God doesn't actually know half as much as he thinks he does...) the strength to pull the child towards her, to embrace him in her arms and hold him close to her chest. Together they sink down and down, still entwined together in beautiful, selfless, precious love as as their souls leave this Earth, journeying across a Broad, Bright, Blue Sky to That Which Lies Beyond.

So it is that God, seeing this one act of beauty, love, compassion and courage, decides that, no, Planet Earth and it's humans shall not be destroyed! There is still hope! My experiment is not a failure! (If I were to play Devil's Advocate I might say that God seized upon the example of Nimah and her baby boy as an excuse not to face up to his responsibilities, but, well...oh, just read on...you'll get my point).

And, far, far away, the Devil, warmly ensconced in his fiery fortress, chuckles to himself (for the Devil knows us much, much better than God, for this is his world, after all) and says...

'Oh my dear, sweet God, you silly, silly, arrogant old fool, you've fallen for their tricks again haven't you...when will you ever learn to admit your mistakes?'

Why The Devil invented The Internet

Once upon a time in the land of Anywhere, in a world long since forgotten, in the fine and prosperous city of Anyplace a handsome young fellow (that being your narrator, obviously), went out for (as you say in your world) ' a night on the tiles'. However, things did not go to plan and by a combination of coincidence, bad judgement and misfortune, I ended up on my own in a pub in a louche and not very respectable (at all!) district of Anywhere known as The Downtown. It was a Friday night, but the place was quiet. I was standing at the bar, just about to order a drink when this guy comes bumbling up to me. A bloke in his fifties (at a guess), he had a florid, greasy complexion and, though skinny, had a strangely swollen belly. To me, he looked, and smelt, like a down-on-his-luck alcoholic. Facially, he bore a remarkable resemblance to a character you would know as Ming the Merciless - from "Flash Gordon."

So, Ming turns to look at me, peering with bloodshot, tired eyes he says "tell you what mate, buy me a drink and I'll tell you a story, a true story, one like you've never 'eard before."

Now, me, I'm a sucker for a story so I'm intrigued, "what sort of story would that be then?" I ask.

"Well, I used to be a clarb driver, din't I and one day I 'ad that Satan in the back of me clarb…" (A 'clarb', by the way, is the Anywhere equivalent of a London black cab).

"Satan? You mean as in the Devil…!?"

"Yeh, that's right, Old Nick 'imself, from The City to The Mansions of The Greedy One Percent, that were the fare and 'e talked the 'ole way, 'e told me stuff, terrible stuff, things I wished I'd never 'eard, stuff that ruined my life."

Okay, I'm hooked. This guy could just be a random nutjob, but the concept of the Devil riding in the back of a clarb and spilling his heart out to the driver is one that's just too good to miss. So, I buy the guy a drink.

And he tells me a story of the Devil.

First off, it's important to note that our Ming was,

before meeting his Satanic customer, just an ordinary clarb driver. Tendency to talk too much, wife, kids, house. After his meeting with Satan, it all fell apart. Wife, kids, house, job, all gone. Too much knowledge is dangerous. For this reason, Ming explained he couldn't tell me everything the Devil told him, or my life, too, would be destroyed. He'd just tell me about things the Devil had invented.

You see Satan has walked with us since we took our first faltering steps in this, and other, existences. In terms of your existence at this moment, He has whispered into the ears of Pol Pot, Genghis Khan, Torquemada and Adolf Hitler. He wielded a machete in Rwanda, dropped napalm in Vietnam and hung "witches" in New England: he has marched with every marauding army that has ever left its blood-stained footprints across countries and continents, he has picked up babies by their legs and dashed their brains out against walls, he has herded women and children into barns, thrown in a phosphorus grenade behind them and bolted shut the doors.

In short, the Devil's a bad sort. He's also a troubled,

deep, contradictory and complex character, for whilst he loathes and detests us (blaming us for his rift with his beloved friend, God), he also loves us. He loves us passionately. He loves us because he was part of our creation and because he is fascinated by us, by our capacity for endless evil. He is amazed that we can give even him a good run for the money in the evil stakes. We constantly delight him: just as he thinks we can't get any worse, we go and do something even nastier. Humans, he has come to believe, have an infinite capacity to do the wrong thing, there is no floor to how low they can go. They are true and fitting disciples for the Swallower of Shadows, the Eater of Souls.

Given his fascination with us, the Devil spends a lot of time down here, wandering around in human form, getting up to all sorts of mischief and generally spreading chaos and misery.

That's what was occurring the day our unfortunate cabby picked up Old Nick in The City (that being the Financial District of Anywhere, the Devil-inspired Ground Zero of all evil). Satan had just been doing a bit of commodities trading, speculating massively in food futures, pushing up the price of basic foodstuffs high enough to ensure that, not many months down the road, children somewhere in the world would starve to death.

So, that roguishly handsome, smartly dressed City type that Ming the cabby picked up that day was not, in fact, a smartly dressed city type, but Satan. And in the course of the journey to The Mansions of The Greedy One Percent he would, being in a particularly good mood that day (having sentenced so many children to death) and feeling particularly loquacious, tell our unfortunate cabby a tale of how the world works that would unhinge the guy's mind forever and leave him a ruined and broken man.

Okay, so, let's get back to the Devil's inventions.

One of the things Satan enjoys doing, besides causing as much grief as possible, is inventing things, things that could be used for good or evil. He invents something new and exciting, whispers it into somebody's ear so that humanity believes the invention is their own. Then he sits back and has a little bet with himself as to whether we'll use his neat little idea for good or for ill. Betting, of course, that we'll use it for the bad.

And the Devil has never lost one of his bets, not ever.

Again, in terms of your own world, a good example of the above would be the Internet. In fact, it's one of Lucifer's proudest inventions – he calls it "a gateway to Hell in every home." Satan knew how we'd use the Internet. True, it's a great way to spread ideas and information, to educate and inform the world. But mostly? Mostly it's a sewer: a forum giving a voice to those who should not have one, a way for government to spy on and manipulate its citizens, a distribution channel for the vilest ideas and images imaginable, a refuge for the impolite, the ignorant, a tool for the huckster, a blessing to the criminal. It desensitises and idiotises us all. It reduces communication to short, intolerant, angry sentences. Eventually it will control and consume us. Just as the Devil planned.

When God and the Devil were Friends

If you're to understand why the Devil invents things then you need to start with one very important fact. And that is that God and The Devil were not always daggers drawn at opposite ends of the spiritual spectrum, so to speak.

Indeed, in the beginning there was the light, and there was God and there was The Devil. And God and The Devil were great friends and partners and the basis, the cement, of that relationship was the world creation business.

Together, God and The Devil would pass many a happy eon together planning and creating new worlds. World after world after world they made together. God would make the basic planet structure, the weather system, the geotectonics and the highest life-form and The Devil would do the rest: the plants, the animals, the insects, the microscopic life. Aware of God's tendency towards 'fire and forget' creation, The Devil, a great believer in post-creation customer support, would then take meticulous care to make sure that each new world created was catalogued, observed and managed, taking the time to tweak and correct any small issues that might come up as the world developed. Thanks to God's creative flair and The Devil's impressive administrative and managerial talents the God-Devil period of world creation was extraordinarily fruitful and the Universe grew at a rate not since matched, with one successful world succeeding another and then another and then another and then...you get the idea. So much different to nowadays when God churns out a world and forgets He's done it, leaving it at the mercy of the forces of entropy – hence the current state of chaos in the Universe, of which I'm sure you're more than well aware of.

All throughout this God-Devil period, The Devil was a delightful creature; warm, friendly, happy, enthusiastic and full of love: not a trace of the evil that was later to consume him. So, what went wrong?

Well, truth be told, it was, as so often, God that made a mess of things.

You see, and this is something you're probably unaware of, God has the attention span of a bored teenager. Here's an example of that easily-distracted mentality of His– the incident that led to The Devil becoming The Devil as you know him today.

So, making successful world after successful world wasn't enough for God. It all became too formulaic for Him and He decided that He would try something new. In all previous worlds made by God and The Devil, the highest life form (as created by Him) operated on a spiritual level governed by one of the Universal Laws of the Universe – that being Love. Now, running a world on that kind of principle is, pretty much, a sure fire recipe for getting it right. But, oh no, that wasn't enough for God, why should He be bound by some silly Universal Law? He was the Supreme Being, after all. Did I mention that God can be a tad arrogant...

The result of God's line of thinking was a plan for a new kind of planet – a planet where the highest life form (codenamed 'humans', a name that remains to this day) would have something that God would call 'free will'. They would be 'free' to decide what was good and what was bad, who to love and who to hate, to be truthful or untruthful and their nature would not be based on the

Universal Law of Love, rather upon whatever rushed in to fill the vacuum.

The Devil, always wise, argued against this. He said it would be a disaster. That it would not work. That it was a recipe for pain and suffering and grief. That there was plenty of bad stuff out there, floating around looking for a home just such as the planet God proposed.

But God, exhibiting now not the characteristics of a bored teenager but of a stuffy, middle-aged, middle class male, decided that He was right, everyone else was wrong and He would do what He jolly well wanted to do and if The Devil didn't like it he could do one. And, after much heated discussion, The Devil went along with God's plan. He recognised that God could be arrogant, spiteful but mostly He was (like us all) a prisoner of His nature and mostly He was good: His sins were sins of omission and frailty and incompetence, not of evil so if God said it would all be okay then he should probably accept that. And after so much time together, so many worlds created together, The Devil had come to love God deeply and found it hard to deny Him anything.

And so a new planet, fully stocked with 'humans' came into existence. And what a disaster it all was! As predicted, Humanity became prey to every poisonous wisp of depravity and evil floating round the Universe. And the Devil, with his micro-management, cataloguing and observation saw it all. For one thousand one hundred and twenty seven years he observed Planet Earth and every day he saw a new atrocity, a new depravity, every day a new crime committed by mankind against mankind or animals or the environment. And The Devil would feel the pain and he would weep. He tried to speak to God about it:

"God, look what your 'humans' are doing – look at the things they do to my beautiful animals, outdone in evil only by the things they do to each other! You must take away this curse of free will or this new planet will become a ball of suppurating evil that will infect the Universe!"

God was having none of it, truth be told he'd already moved on to the next thing and had completely forgotten about creating Planet Earth and the whole 'free will' thing (a concept he, thankfully, used only once) and, anyway, he was the Supreme Being so what was The Devil talking about? Supreme Beings don't make mistakes. Things became very tense between God and The Devil, The Devil depressed and outraged on a day by day basis by the horrors of God's new planet and infuriated by God's indifference to it all and refusal to engage. Eventually The Devil could bear his pain and frustration no longer and resolved to solve the problem himself. One day, whilst God was off doing Supreme Being type things, he hacked into the new planet's Life Forms Database and accessed humanity's DNA. His attention was to splice out those baleful chromosomes responsible for free will. Oh, if he had succeeded in the plan what a better place your world would be today! But – sadly for all concerned some particularly obsequious and nosey Archangel spotted what The Devil was up to and reported the matter to God.

And God was furious!

How dare anyone interfere with His creation!

Who, exactly, is the Supreme Being around here!

No-one, but no-one, challenges the Authority of God!

And so The Devil's gallant attempt to free humanity of the curse of free will failed. God and The Devil fought terribly. God was maddened with rage. Rather than argue more, rather than accept The Devil's, frankly very coherent, assessment of the situation, rather than admit that He had made a mistake, God went big time Old Testament and yelled:

"If you're that bothered about that bloody planet you can bloody well go and live there – you're bloody well banished!"

The next thing The Devil knew he was there on that horrible mistake of a planet. Alone. Banished. Denied the love of God and all that he had ever known and cherished. His poor heart broke into a thousand pieces and he cried and cried for a precious and beautiful thing lost and never to be found again.

For the next one thousand one hundred and forty three years, The Devil wandered the face of the planet of his banishment, a poor lost soul mourning his break with God, but despite his own pain he was still, at that stage, a creature filled with love and he would try and share it with humans whenever he met them. He was constantly rebuffed, cast out, laughed at and ridiculed. He became filled with despair and, eventually and to his horror, he noticed evil thoughts sneaking into his own mind. At first it was just one at a time, then two, then three, then a multitude until he knew that the evil of humanity was infecting him, too, that it was gnawing and eating away at everything good in his soul.

Then there arrived the black day when the power of evil that had crept into him became too strong. Chancing upon a random and vulnerable person The Devil - in a fashion that is all too human - committed an unspeakable and vile atrocity against that person.

What had he become? A monster. He was corrupted. A threshold had been crossed. Deeply distressed, The Devil roared at the sky, unleashing a cry so loud that it shook mountains and of such bleakness that it killed babies in the womb. The Devil was ashamed of what he'd done, disgusted by what he'd become. In his shame, he wished to hide his face from God. So he began to dig into the ground beneath his feet. He dug and he dug, down and down. Down to the molten bowels of the planet. And there he would make his home.

The Devil had hoped that burying himself so deep down would protect him from the evil of people. But it was not to be. Evil carried on infecting The Devil, taking over his soul and becoming to him as addictive as any powerful drug. He began to revel and delight in the power of evil and where once he had tried to spread Love he now spread hate and pain and suffering, seeking to always increase the Greater Sum of Misery in the Universe. And when an evil soul left a human body he would gather it to himself in his fiery home, Hell as he had christened it, both to draw strength from its evil and to punish it for its role in making him the wretched creature he had become. So, you see, the Devil is a creation not of himself but of God's pettiness and humanity's evil – but whilst drawn to that evil, he still seeks to punish it. Just as God is not entirely good, The Devil is not entirely bad.

The Greatest Love of All

There was once an Angel and this Angel was somewhat confused as to the nature of Love, in particular what exactly was 'The Greatest Love of All.'

So, naturally, the Angel sought help from The Font of all Wisdom, God.

And the Angel went before God and he asked, 'God, I humbly ask, what truly is The Greatest Love of All?'

'Is it a mother's love for her children?'

And God said, 'no.'

'Is it a father's love for his children?'

And God said, 'no.'

'Is it a child's love for his or her parents?'

And God said, 'no.'

'Is it the love between brothers and sisters?'

And God said, 'no.'

'Is it the love between best friends?'

And God said, 'no.'

'Is it, then, the love between a couple who have spent a life time together?'

And God said, 'no.'

'Uhm – could it be the love for one's neighbour…perhaps…maybe…?'

And still God said 'no.'

'Then, honestly, Lord, I must say I am mightily confused…'

'In that case, Angel,' replied God 'let me enlighten you. The Greatest Love of All is that of the Good Samaritan for he crossed the road to help someone of whom he knew nothing, with whom he had no connection and without any expectation of anything in return. Of all kinds of Love, this is true friendship and friendship The Greatest Love Of All.

And the Devil, deep down in his fiery fortress, saw this exchange between Angel and Supreme Being, chuckled sardonically, shook his massively be-horned Satanic head and said to himself…"hah, so what is that you actually know, oh blessed God…in all your smug, callous, arrogance…of love and friendship; exactly where were you when I needed you?"

Good Friend or Bad Friend?

Once upon a time in the land of Anywhere, in a world long since forgotten, in the fine and prosperous city of Anyplace The Devil was strolling through The Park of a Thousnad Joyous Souls. This particular day, The Devil was in human form – something he often does as he so enjoys mixing among humans and spreading as much misery and chaos as possible. Today he was well-groomed and smartly dressed, for he was on his way to a meeting with a cabal of Pyschopathic Billionaires (who, through their tame politicians and completely owned Means of Communications, were the real rulers of Anywhere) to present them with a plan.

What exactly The Devil's plan was is really relevant to this tale (though needless to say it would result in rich, evil old men becoming even richer - and eviler – and The Ordinary Folk becoming even poorer).

No, the plan doesn't matter. What matters is this...

For something stopped The Devil in his tracks – a little girl sitting alone on a bench, crying to herself. The

Devil, turned, looked at the little girl and suddenly, that was it. The sound and sight of one so innocent in such distress suddenly shocked him back to the creature he once was when he and God were still friends and before he was infected with the Evil of Humans – a being of love, grace and care.

Unable to help himself, Satan sat on the bench besides the crying girl and said, 'child, why are you crying like this, you're far too young to be so sad...tell me what has upset you so?'

The little girl lifted her head out of her hands and looked up at this strange man who was suddenly talking to her and she saw not The Devil but somebody who looked like they really cared...'it was my friend...', she said...'my mum bought me a new dress and I wore it today and she said I looked fat and stupid in it and ugly and I thought she was my friend but she's not my friend..'

'Hold on little girl....two things.....first is that you are not, never have been and never will be ugly...it's not up to others to define what or who you are, ignore them. You were born in and of the Stars and travelled an eternity to be here in this world. When you were making that journey God saw you and he was so moved by your beauty that he tore off a piece of himself and placed it inside you...you call that piece of God inside you your Soul. Now given that, little girl, given you are made from the very Stars and a piece of God Himself, well, the very idea that you are anything but a thing of stunning beauty is nonsense, is it not? Hah! The second thing, well the second thing is very, very important. You must learn in life to distinguish between A Good Friend and A Bad Friend. Let me explain'...

'Truth is, my child, that as you grow to be even bigger and more grown up than you are now, you'll realise that none of us are in as much control of our lives as we like to think we are. So much of what happens to us happens because of chance and coincidence and that chance and coincidence is decided by The Blind Old Weaver Of Fate as She spins together the cloth that makes up the story of our lives. Next to her, by her spinning wheel, sits a huge pile of jumbled thread and from this pile she picks – at random, for She is blind, after all – the threads that she will weave together to spin our stories. Some of these *threads are white, some silver, some gold and some black. The white threads represents days that are, well, just ordinary, neither good nor bad – the kind of days that will make up most of our lives. The silver threads are good days, the kind of days that are full of laughter and friendship, the kind of days that leave you with a smile on your face. The gold threads represent exceptional and rare days, days of success and achievement, pure triumph even, and days of magic like getting married or having a baby. The black threads, though...ahh...the black threads...the black threads are the bad days, days of desolation, despair, loss – the kind of days that steal your breath, that crush and compress and suffocate and squeeze hope out of your soul. It's when you have these 'black thread' days – and, my daughter, you will have these days, when they come be strong and remember they will pass - that you'll discover if a friend is really a friend.*

You see, a true friend is someone who loves and cares for you and who will stick with you through good and bad. A friend who is not real is someone who is your 'friend' only because you amuse them or because they feel they can get something from you – as soon as things are bad for you, when you have those black thread days, these false friends will show themselves to be false by what they say.

For if you are struggling in life a good friend will say things like:

'Anytime you need to talk, just let me know…'

'I'm your friend, I'm here for you, always…'

'These things happen to us all, you'll be fine…'

'What can I do to help…'

'I understand…'

But a 'friend' who is really no friend at all will say:

'I told you so…'

'Well, what do you expect…'

'You should have done this…you should have done that…'

'You need to go on medication…'

'Really, it's your own fault…'

'Whatever…anyway, let's talk about me…'

'Sorry…I'm far too busy to talk now…'

Throughout her life, The girl was well served by the Devil's advice on the subject of friends and when she found a friend who responded to the 'black threads' in her life like a true friend she would cherish them and hold them dear and when she found a 'friend' to be nothing more than a selfish person out only for what they could get, she cut them out of her life as she would a malignant cancer from her body.

And the motto of this story is exactly as it 'says on tin'; when the going gets tough your pretend friends get gone but your real friends reveal themselves in their actions and words.

FakeBook

Once upon a time...in the land of Anywhere, in a world long since forgotten, in the fine and prosperous city of Anyplace, a clever but amoral man working for the Greedy One Percent hit upon an excellent way of exerting control over the masses and reinforcing the power of The System (actually, he didn't 'hit upon' anything, it was, as you now know, another case of the Devil planting an evil seed of an evil invention in a human mind). His idea was a form of Social Control (which in your world you call Social Media) and it was called FakeBook.

The man's Greedy One Percent employer's soon recognised the potential of FakeBook to control the way The Ordinary Folk thought and using the Secret Powers of Advertising and Celebrity Endorsement, FakeBook was Constantly Hyped as something which should be In Every Home and on which everyone should have a Profile.

And so it came to pass that soon FakeBook was in every home and everyone did indeed have a profile.

Soon, the populace of Anywhere fell into FakeBook Groupthink as only Government Approved Views were allowed expression on FakeBook; a policy reinforced by millions of Fake FakeBook Accounts controlled by the Government (and by The Government I, of course, mean The Greedy One Percent). The Fake FakeBook accounts spewed out Government Sanctioned Propaganda and launched Vicious Personal Attacks on anybody expressing a Non-Sanctioned Point Of View (before their Non-Sanctioned Point of View posts were deleted by the FakeBook Controllers).

FakeBook was a spectacular success and The Ordinary Folk now thought only in terms of FakeBook Groupthink. If it wasn't on FakeBook it wasn't happening and if FakeBook said something was true (even if it was a Big Lie) then it was true and if FakeBook said you had to do something, well then, you just had to do it, didn't you?

If you asked Johnny "why did you say that, Johnny? That's a terrible thing to say to someone," Johnny would reply, "because everyone else on FakeBook was saying it."

If you asked Johnny "why do you believe that, Johnny, there's absolutely no evidence that that is so?" Johnny would reply "you're wrong, it is true because FakeBook says it is true, how dare you question The Truth!"

If you asked Johnny "oh, Johnny, why oh why did you kill your friend?" Johnny would reply "because I wanted to broadcast his murder on FakeBookLive and get lots of 'likes'."

And the moral of this tale is...delete your social media accounts, life will be better without them; social media has nothing positive to offer, it's a sewer of manipulation, lies, depravity and cruelty.

Poor Man, Rich Man

Once upon a time in the land of Anywhere, in a world long since forgotten, in the fine and prosperous city of Anyplace, a Poor Man was walking to work. Now this man lived in a run-down flat in one of the deprived zones that encircle the bustling financial district of Anywhere, the City, and to get to his place of work (for he was employed in a nearby branch of McSlurry) he had to cross the thriving hub of finance.

So there he was, a Poor Man dressed in cheap clothes, strolling along the affluent pathways of this wealthy area. As he walked, he whistled, for the sun was bright and the sky was blue and there was happiness in his Soul.

Coming in the opposite direction, walking towards the Poor Man, was a Rich Man. He was a trader in the new financial product that had taken the City by storm in recent months, the HORFIOD (Highly Opaque and Risky Financial Instrument Of Death) and, as such, was a member of the families of The One Percent and lived, like the rest of his kind, in a fine house in one of the best parts of Anywhere.

Now today was not a good day for the Rich Man as he was particularly weighed down with the troubles and cares of wealth and was running frantically from business meeting to business meeting and he was not happy, not happy at all.

He was somewhat affronted, then, to see the Poor Man. After all, here was this chap coming down the street towards him, smiling, whistling and obviously in love with the world, yet from his demeanour and cheap clothes he was equally obviously a Poor Man of no means and no money. What right had he to be so offensively cheerful? What possible cause could he have to be so happy? Unacceptable! He determined that he would find out what was going on with this strange fellow, this insolent Poor Person

With this thought upon his mind and being by now in a very bad mood, the Rich Man, upon drawing level with the Poor Man said, "You, Poor Man, stop!"

And the Poor Man stopped, looked the Rich Man in the eye and, smiling in an infuriatingly pleasant way replied, "of course, sir, how may I help you?"

"Well, I'll come straight to the point. I found your obvious happiness an effrontery and most annoying and I wish you immediately to cease smiling and stop whistling. You have no right to be happy, I can tell simply from looking at you that you're a man without money and means and as such your position in life should be one of abject misery and I demand that you behave in a manner fitting and appropriate to your miserable station in life!"

"But, sir," replied the Poor Man, "respectful of your authority and all as I am, I have to beg to differ. You're right, of course, that money is a constant worry but I have a roof over my head and food on the table and a job of work. I have a wife who I love very much and who loves me and I have two beautiful, healthy children who are the apple of my eye…these things are Jewels Beyond Price."

"Jewels Beyond Price! Hah! What balderdash! Why, my fine house has twenty bedrooms and the largest of these is bigger, I'll wager, than the entire hovel in which you no doubt live."

"Then, sir, I'm sure you would win that bet for my home is humble indeed, but it is a happy home and that is enough for me"

"Ah, you fool! My wife is a former model and beautiful beyond compare, the kind of woman you most assuredly could not afford! Your own wife, I'm sure, is some fat, frumpy old fishwife and a pain to the eye."

"But, sir, I love my wife as my life itself, as she does me. Every time I look at her I see the most beautiful woman in the world and that is more than enough for me."

"What an idiot you are Poor Person! Why my children have the best of everything, they want for nothing, what do *your* mewling brats have?"

"Well, sir, it'd be true to say my children do not have as many...things...as yours but they are fed and clothed, loved and protected and encouraged in all they do and every night as I kiss them in their beds as they lay sleeping I see that they are smiling contentedly and that is certainly enough for me."

"Hah! What a pathetic Poor Fool you are, you understand nothing. I am a powerful and feared man, and what are you…I mean, look at you…who would ever fear you!"

"No, sir, I am not feared, nor would I want to be, I am happier having the good friends I have who like me for being me, not because they fear me."

"Moron! Fool! Imbecile! Look, let me put this in simple terms that even someone as impoverished and brainless as yourself would understand. I have *more* than you and this time next year I will have *even more* than you and the year after that I will have *more again* and the next year I will have *still more* than you and so on and so on until I have everything and you have nothing! There, now what do you say to that you scummy peasant!?"

"Sir, I can only say once again that I am blessed in what I do have, I do not like to waste my time worrying about what I do not have. Why would I want more when I already have enough?"

"Harrumph!" Harrumphed the Rich Man and, concluding, in sheer frustration, that there was no reasoning with this insolent fool of a man, span on his heel and walked away, leaving the Poor Man to continue his journey.

What a deluded idiot! Good grief! thought the Rich man. '*Why would I want more,*' indeed! *How stupid; after all, one always wants more, getting more is the point of everything. What kind of life can one have if one doesn't have more?* And yet…he could still hear that stubborn, insolent, stupid, *happy* Poor Man whistling as he walked away down the street. Happy? Nonsense! Love? Nonsense! Children? Nonsense! Happiness is money and then more money. Plain and simple.

But with that thought, something strange happened to the Rich Man. Maybe it happened because he was having a bad day, too much stress, too much to do, or maybe it happened because a mischievous and malignant Devil is always ready to sharply remind us of who we really are.

Whatever the cause, the Rich Man was suddenly struck by an intense bout of insight: something which people of his class and wealth are normally blissfully free of. He saw his life for what it was. His pretty, younger wife. Married not for love, but as a trophy. He didn't love her. And she didn't love him, not for a minute, his touch repulsed her. But she did love the money, the clothes, the parties, the house and the jewels. And as for the two children: they were far from being the apple of his eye. In fact he barely knew them, certainly didn't love them: they were just something that had to be produced by a man in his position; to his wife, giving birth to them was part of the financial contract that was their marriage. Raised by nannies and governesses, his children were growing up unloved and unwanted and would become troubled and difficult adults. And that big, beautiful house of his? Upon reflection it was big but not beautiful; rather, a cold, empty space devoid of meaning and feeling.

All he had was money. Lots and lots of money. But money can't share a joke or a confidence with you; it cannot be your friend. It cannot hold your hand, or kiss you or hold you near.

With this shock of insight the Rich Man suddenly felt very alone. He felt a sense of rising panic and anxiety, of sorrow and loss. He stopped walking. He felt hot and sick and dizzy and…and at that point his heart, weakened by years of stress and rich living, decided to give up the struggle and ceased to beat.

The Rich Man fell to the ground, aware of an absence of motion in his chest and an inability to breathe. This was it, he was dying! But this could not be, for surely he was Too Rich To Die?

And just before the Rich Man made the final journey from this world to the other, his insight suddenly widened further and he had a vision of the very inside of his Soul, and his last living feelings were ones of endless and deep despair. He saw his Soul for what it was: a vast, empty, barren desert in which there was not a living thing except a myriad rats, scuttling pointlessly and desperately back and forth in search of something they didn't even know they were looking for and would never find, and across the thick, black fur of each of these rats was emblazoned, in blood red capital letters, the word GREED.

At this point the Rich Man's existence slipped into the dense Fog Of Forgotten Stories which makes up so much of history and his Soul passed into the possession of He who had always really owned it – He who had bought it for the price of meaningless bling and shiny baubles of Earthly wealth - the Swallower of Souls, the Devil.

Why did the Devil invent Religion?

When God created us, he gave us all the Innate Ability (should we choose to use it – that pesky 'free will' thing that God so foolishly came up with, remember?) of Faith. Now here's the crucial point. There is a massive difference between Faith and Religion. Faith is the God-given gift to have a direct relationship with God himself: no-one else involved in that, just you and God talking and relating, as God intended (allegedly).

The Devil always considered this whole 'Faith' thing to be quite silly – another example of God's over-whelming arrogance; to the Devil 'Faith' is simply God telling humanity. 'you must worship me because I like the praise and the subservience because I am, after all, *the* Supreme Being. Don't expect anything in return though as I'm far to busy creating stuff to give a stuff!'

But...forgive me, I digress, let's carry on with this little tale about religion...because the Devil pondered God's concept of Faith and thought to himself 'hey, God, you've come up with this 'Faith' thing. Thanks for that and if you don't mind I'm going to, er, *finesse*, it a bit'...

So, if 'Faith' is about you having a relationship (of a kind) with God, then Religion is a Devil-created construct that seeks to put a middle-man in the way of your relationship with God. That way the relationship can be distorted and twisted and the "middle-man" is in a position of power and influence; the Devil knows all too well that any man or woman in a powerful position will eventually become corrupted by it. And from corruption, like Water From A Spring, comes Evil, which is exactly why the Devil came up with the concept of religion – he though it would be a marvellous way to sow division, grief, despair and death amongst humanity.

And off goes the Devil, whispers his little plan in the ears of a few talented and unscrupulous individuals and steps back to see how this particular little virus develops…

Initially success was limited. Humankind came up with what we know as Paganism. Okay, it disrupted communication with God but to the Devil's tastes it just wasn't, well, virulent enough. The Devil had hoped that as well as destroying a Faith based relationship with God, religion would also become a huge force for evil and conflict in itself as Competing Religions fought each other for Power And Influence and persecuted those who believed differently to themselves.

Unfortunately Pagan religions rubbed along, on the whole, pretty well with one another, generally accepted each others beliefs and were not, in the Devil's opinion, sufficiently sexist, racist and homophobia.

Back to the drawing board then.

The Devil sat back and brooded for a few centuries and the suddenly, he hit on a real doozy of an idea.

He would create, over a period of time, three similar but competing religions. One he would call Judaism, another Christianity and another Islam.

He personally would micro-manage each Religion. He would ensure that each would spread across the world and that each would be dosed with liberal helpings not only of racism-ramped-up-to-genocidal-max, sexism, and homophobia but would also instil a moral code into its believers that could never be lived up to and believe completely that only it was the One And True Religion, the Only Route To God and that each was free to commit any and every atrocity in the name of God that it felt necessary to uphold its position.

And was the Devil right? Was his plan a success? You betcha! His idea has unleashed centuries of suffering and bloodshed upon the human race, a tide of Religion-Inspired Misery that still spreads its Message Of Death And Despair around the world to this day.

Ladies and Gentlemen, I present to you the Devil's proudest invention: Religion.

What If?

What if a single act of kindness could have more power than all the money in the world?

What if this life is but one step in a much longer journey?

What if you are special and unique but no more special or unique than anyone else?

What if all that you can see isn't all there is to be seen?

What if courage comes in more forms than society cares to admit?

What if the most powerful force in the Universe is Love?

What if Love really doesn't give a damn who you love?

What if success isn't actually defined by how much shiny bling you own?

What if difference is a profound strength rather than something to be mocked?

What if real friends are flesh and blood, not social media profiles?

What if you're defined not by race or colour, gender or

sexuality, religion or belie f but simply by your shared humanity.

What if you are so much more than just mud and sea water seasoned with a hint of consciousness?

Things The Devil DIDN'T invent

Are there more Devil's Inventions? Wow, yes, you betcha. Far more than I can write about here and far more than you want to know about if you wish to preserve your sanity – there's 'The Devil's Book of the Dead' for example which...no...I'm sorry...I've hinted at it in an earlier Tale but telling you of it's full evil grotesqueness? No. I just won't go there...and you don't want to know, really, trust me. Let's concentrate instead on what the Devil didn't invent, because it's the stuff he didn't come up with that actually tells us far more about our relationship with him, and why he loves us so, than the stuff he did come up with.

So...the Devil DIDN'T invent: murder, rape, child abuse, cruelty, torture, bigotry, racism, sexism hatred, stupidity, selfishness, bankers, politicians, billionaires, buy-to-let-landlords, guns, nuclear weapons, war, austerity, globalisation, zero hours contracts, neo-liberalism, oligarchs, Big Pharma, insecticides, 5G, Marvel Superheroes, 'celebrities', cancel culture, divide and conquer identity politics, starvation in a world of plenty, ecosystem destruction, smartphones, dead bees, privatisation, hunting, bull-fighting, industrial farming, the corporate media, propaganda, pollution, privilege, class, cheating, lying, stealing, betrayal, homelessness, misery, destitution, despair, corporations, predatory capitalism, 'growth forever' economics, fast fashion, slavery, sex trafficking, human organ trading, social media 'influencers', ignorance, corruption, greed, inequality, obscene wealth, poverty, terrorism, counter terrorism, responsibility to protect, regime change, biological warfare, deforestation, genetic modification, genocide....oh no, we did all these and shitloads more without any help at all from the Devil – which is, of course, why he loves us so.

And in our next little tale, the dark, dark story of The Factory, you'll see exactly how humans do not need Satan to create their own horrifying vision of Hell on Earth....

The Factory

Once upon a time…in the land of Anywhere, in a world long since forgotten, in the fine and prosperous city of Anyplace there was a Corporation that was much admired and respected by the Greedy One Percent for it was generally agreed that this Corporation had led the way in process of 'worldization' – this being the process by which Corporations had sacked people making their products in the land of Anywhere for a decent, living wage and given their work, instead, to slaves in Faraway, poverty-struck lands. This process, by removing the cost of paying fairly for honest labour, had a magnificent effect on Profit Margins and became quite the thing to do. Of course, the long term effect of such a process, obvious to me and you, would be that eventually there would be no-one earning any money to buy the cheap tat made by the Corporations slave labour workforce but, remember, we are ruled by psychopaths and psychopaths do not see the long term consequences of their actions, they seek only to satisfy (and are blinded by) their Short Term Greed.

Anyway, back to our Corporation. Recently it had become even more admired and respected amongst The Greedy One Percent because of the way it ran its main production facility – The Factory. The Factory was a huge…well…factory, in a Faraway Land where the Corporation made most of its Tat (in this case that Tat was iDiotphones).

The Factory was so well respected (envied, even) by The Greedy One Percent because it was regarded as an almost perfect example of Worldization at its best – everything about it was about Minimising Cost and Maximising Revenue.

This is how The Factory worked.

The Faraway Land in which it was based was desperately poor. The managers of The Factory would approach parents in that country and offer them a sum of money to Apprentice their children into employment in The Factory (The Factory only employed children as they were more malleable than adults and their Small and Nimble fingers were particularly adept at assembling iDiotphones). Parents would readily agree to these apprenticeships as they were desperate for income and one less mouth to feed – they also believed the Glossy Promotional Materials of The Factory that implied (though such implication shall not be taken at any time as explicit promise of such…) they were apprenticing their children into a Marvellous Career that was Full Of Opportunity and possible Promotion to Managerial Responsibility.

None of what the children's parents were told was true. Working in The Factory was not an 'opportunity'. It was a death sentence.

Upon arrival at The Factory it was explained to the children (who may or may not have understood, who cares) that the money paid to their parents for their 'apprenticeship' was actually a loan. A loan the children had to repay, with a four figure sum of Compound Interest added on monthly. Until that loan was repaid the children were Property of The Factory and would live, sleep eat and work there until such time as the loan was cleared. But given that wages at The Factory were derisory, that deductions were made for accommodation, food, uniforms and 'training' plus the huge monthly charge for Compound Interest. Well. Given all that, the loan would of course NEVER be repaid and the children would, in fact, remain in debt to The Factory and Property of The Factory from the day they arrived there until the day they died.

Not that Death would be long in coming…

Now we come to the nitty-gritty of why The Factory was so widely admired and envied and was so successful at Minimising Cost and Maximising Revenue; The Factory knew how to Sweat Its Assets…those being, primarily, its child labour workforce.

After a brief 'training' period, new child recruits (some as young as eight years old) would be put to work on the production line, slotting together components to create iDiotphone after iDiotphone. The children would stand, not sit, at the production line for nineteen hours a day, day after day, seven days a week. They would stand on a floor that was a metal grill, thus negating the need for toilet breaks as the children could do the necessary where they stood - their piss and shit dripping and dropping through the grilled floor to be drained away. Talking was forbidden and Supervisors would savagely beat any child who broke this rule, as they would also beat any child deemed to be working to slowly, or making too many mistakes or just because, hey, I can't beat you if I want to so that's what I'm going to do. Food would be bought to them as they worked. They had three minutes, three minutes exactly, to wolf it down. The 'food' they were given barely qualified as such, it in fact being rendered chicken faeces (politely known as 'chicken digest' – you can find it in many dry pet foods in your world), a by-product of the many huge chicken battery-farms that had recently been set up in this Faraway Land by the same Corporation that owned The Factory.

At the end of their nineteen hour shifts the hapless, hopeless, doomed children were herded into massive, bare, unheated sheds where they were expected to sleep, before being woken just a few hours later to begin another shift on the iDiotphone production line.

Taking into account the children's long hours, and the fact they were never in fact paid any wages (due to deductions, Compound Interest, accommodation charges etc.), the Cost Of Labour as a Contribution To Costs in The factory was very small, a fact to put a bring a huge smile to the Ugly Face of any Greedy One Percenter. But things got better. The factory had, in fact, found a way to not only have its workforce work practically for free but to actually turn it into a Profit Centre.

How did The Factory do this? What follows is not pleasant, but it is necessary, so bear with me...

I mentioned before that the children working in The Factory were doomed. I meant this quite literally. A combination of long hours, brutality, lack of sleep, bad diet, disease, accident, illness and non-existent medical facilities or health care meant that no child survived for more two years in The Factory. There were plenty of new children to buy in poverty-stricken Faraway Land so this was not seen as a problem. In fact, the child's death was a necessary part of the way The Factory functioned, and was the point at which that child stopped being a Labour Cost and was turned into a Profit Centre.

For when a child died its body was taken to a separate facility within The Factory, one which could best be compared to an abattoir in your own world. Within this facility/abattoir huge machines stripped the child's body of skin, flesh and organs. This horrible mixture that was once a human being was transported by long conveyor belts to a huge mincing machine which reduced skin, flesh, internal organs, heart, brains, eyes, intestines – everything - to a fine mince. This mince (being at this stage an odd and unappetising colour) was then bleached, dyed a 'meat-type colour' and shaped into quarter pound 'beef' burgers. These burgers were then shipped back to the land of Anywhere to be sold in the famous Slurry burger chain (also owned by the same Corporation that owned the factory). Brilliant, no? A most comprehensive Sweating of an Asset, is it not?

Aha, but what about the bones, I hear you say? Don't worry, these too were used profitably for when the child's skeleton had been picked clean of all flesh it was sent on another long conveyor belt on a journey that would end in a massive crusher that pulverised the bones to a fine dust. That dust was then labelled as 'flour' and shipped back to the land of Anywhere, to be used in the baking of the famous cupcakes sold in the equally famous Sickbuckets chain of cake and coffee shops.

Happily for the children of Faraway Land, The Factory closed its doors when the land of Anywhere collapsed under the weight of the depredations of The Greedy One Percent and the fatal contradictions inherent in 'worldization'. Unhappily for you, The Factory (and many, many other factories just like it) is now up and running in your own world, in a land not that far away.

The Devil's Special Child

Once upon a time… many, many years ago in a world long since forgotten, there was a country called Anywhere. And in the land of Anywhere there was a fine and prosperous city called Anyplace and in this city there lived, during the times of the ascendancy of the destructive and rapist Greedy One Percent, a politician called Bonty Liar.

Now Bonty was a hugely corrupt man, most definitely one of the Devil's Special Children. From a well-to-do family, he had been educated at one of the Finest Public Schools in the land of Anywhere, benefiting from the Best Education Money Can Buy.

From school, with help from Friends Of His Father, he entered the legal profession and soon, by dint of the fact that he was a good actor, an adept liar and lacking in social or moral conscious he, not surprisingly, did very well in his chosen career and was soon a Promising Young Lawyer.

It was at the Promising Young Lawyer stage that he was spotted by members of The Greedy One Percent, who were always on the lookout for bright, morality-free, personable young men and women they could manoeuvre into positions of Responsibility And Power.

And so the inducements began. Having a Feral Ability to sniff out Bad Character, The Greedy One Percent recognised Bonty's dysfunctionally and strange sense of self-regard, his greed for money and power and sociopathic tendencies and suggested to him that he might enter the World Of Politics where, should he but do their bidding, he could be very useful to them and they could offer to him in return fame, power and lots and lots of money: a huge advance for a book of his memoirs at a later point in the future, a Guaranteed Income Stream from speaking tours (addressing members of The One Percent), lucratively paid non-executive directorships on the boards of Banks And Corporations, well-rewarded contracts to write articles for The Means Of Communication...these were just some of the inducements offered to Bonty to do The One Percent's bidding.

Bonty accepted everything offered gladly: he was, and always had been, fascinated by the extremely wealthy and was desperate to join their ranks.

Mentored by The One Percent, quietly supported by their money and noisily supported by their tame journalists in The Means Of Communication, Bonty rose quickly in the Political Sphere, soon becoming Leader of his party and then Leader Of The Country.

Bonty now proved his worth to The Greedy One Percent. If a law needed changing or abrogating to allow them to pursue a business that had previously been seen as unconscionable or illegal, Bonty changed it. If a (rare as Trolls teeth) honest politician or journalist needed to be blackmailed or bludgeoned into silence, Bonty wielded the club. If corrupt policy had to be justified by lies, Bonty lied. If the Public Services or Benefits And Welfare had to be cut to impoverish The Ordinary Folk, Bonty did the cutting. If an Illegal War needed to be started in a Far Flung Land to enable The Greedy One Percent to steal that land's resources and make even more money selling arms...well, Bonty started it.

In short, Bonty proved to be an Invaluable Servant of The Greedy One Percent. If anything, they came to realise that they had, in fact, underestimated his greed for money and power and the depths of his sociopathic leanings: Bonty not only did what they wanted but during the course of his ten years as Leader, he managed to prostitute the entire Office Of Leadership to the sole purpose of enriching himself and his Owners.

I suppose it could be argued that The Ordinary Folk of Anywhere had some blame in the rise of Bonty Liar. Perhaps they should have noticed the blindingly obvious fact that his surname was LIAR or perhaps they should have realised that his infuriating habit of smiling whenever he was talking was in fact a form of "Distraction Theft;" the cheesy grin distracting your eye whilst hands sneak round the back of you and steal your wallet, your Life Chances and the lives of your children. I suppose I would then have to say, how can people make informed decisions when The Means Of Communication function as a 24 hour, 7 day a week, 365 days a year Propaganda Mouthpiece for the wealthy and powerful?

Whatever the rights and wrongs and who was to blame, Bonty accumulated vast amounts of Blood And Treasure and became a happy man. And if his incredible success was built on the deaths of hundreds of thousands of people in Far Flung Foreign Lands and the impoverishment of others in his own country…well, then, what of it. You Ordinary Folk are but a detail of history.

Now one particular day, three years after stepping down as Leader Of The Country, Bonty (now an immensely wealthy non-executive director of numerous corporations and banks, columnist, after dinner speaker, author, property investor and, irony of ironies, Peace Envoy) was giving a speech (for a very nice fee) to a Select Group of Greedy One Percent Individuals. Comfortable and pompous, he stood there on stage, pontificating from behind a lectern. Then something very, very strange happened.

Bonty had spent a good half hour lauding the Wonderful And Generous Nature of the fabulously Wealthy and their Inestimable Contribution To The Nation, extolling the virtues of the Magick of "Trickle Down" theory and was just about to start telling a series of Vile Lies about the Leader of a Far Flung Foreign land, that being to lay the ground work for Propaganda in the next day's Means Of Communication that would eventually become justification for another Illegal War, when his Soul decided it had had enough.

For, oddly, despite spending a lifetime in Bonty's corrupt body, his Soul had remained Pure, close to God and In Equilibrium With The Universe. But as it saw yet more Filth And Lies coming down from Bonty's diseased and crazed mind, filth aimed at starting yet another war in which yet more Innocents would die, his Soul decided enough was enough. It had always tried to do its God-Given duty, had spent decades telling Bonty, No Don't Do That Its Horrible. Always it had been ignored, always squeezed out by Bonty's lust for money and power, by his complete lack of regard for others. It was time to accept defeat and save itself from the Rampant Corruption that this man, this Child Of The Devil, represented. It was off, it was out of here and on to That Which Lies Beyond, Sod This For A Game Of Soldiers.

As Bonty uttered the first of his lies about the Leader of the Far Flung Foreign Land, his face became very red.

Sweat broke out on his forehead and poured down his face, he paused as he spoke, discomfited by the intense heat that seemed to have flared up inside himself. Then he moaned in pain as more heat bubbled up from somewhere deep, deep down and steam came off him in great waves, he rolled his head back and screamed as his eyes turned all white, like an egg yolk being boiled... clouds of smoke billowed from his mouth, nostrils and ears and he suddenly, and explosively, burst into flames, fire consuming his body as he stood at his lectern.

Terrified by such a spectacle, his Rich Guests ran screaming from the room, sparing them the site of Bonty's flaming head exploding into tiny fragments as his Soul made its exit from his Vile Body, a fast-moving Incandescence, shooting upwards, smashing through the nearest window, out into Fresh And Sweet Air and making its escape across a Broad, Bright Blue Sky.

What was left of Bonty's body collapsed to the floor, lying smouldering by the lectern, and at that point the ground around began to shake and tremor and a large hole opened up in the ground by Bonty's remains. It was hole so deep that it reached down to Hell itself and from it issued Flame and the Nauseating Smell of Brimstone, and out of the Hole crept a Large, Scaly, Red Hand which snatched away the remains of Bonty and dragged them down to Hell: the hand of the Devil himself, come to reclaim one of his Special Children.

And the moral of this tale is: never trust those who seek to put themselves in positions of authority above you. Most of them are strange and twisted people, often sociopaths, thieves and rapists, and they seek only to benefit themselves and their dark desires.

A Mountain of a Million Corpses

This short piece is dedicated to Bonty Liar...

I am a man of power and influence. And I've climbed a mountain of a million corpses to get here.

I am a man of fame, known the world over. And I've climbed a mountain of a million corpses to get here.

I am a man who knows Popes and Presidents. And I've climbed a mountain of a million corpses to get here.

I am a man of Faith and Religion. And I've climbed a mountain of a million corpses to get here.

I am a man who has a place in history. And I've climbed a mountain of a million corpses to get here.

I am a man who regrets nothing, for I know I am right. And I've climbed a mountain of a million corpses to get here.

I am a man of huge wealth, owner of many properties. And I've climbed a mountain of a million corpses to get here.

I am a man who has built an Empire and its foundations are the Blood And Bones Of Innocents, for I have built a mountain of a million corpses to get here.

Why The Devil invented 4.02A.M.

This particular Devil's Invention, as related to me that night in Soho by Ming, the sad and broken clarby, is not cultural or technological but falls firmly into "the other" category and is a good example of how relentlessly And viciously evil the Devil is.

Let me, then, tell you the story of a particular time of the day invented by Satan, in terms of the clock you use in your world; this time would correspond to two minutes past four in the morning.

It's a scientific and medical fact that more people die at 4.02am than at any other time. Scientists and doctors explain this away by saying that this is the exact time when our bio-rhythms are at their lowest. Whilst that's completely correct, it's also a simplistic, three dimensional explanation posited by people who are limited in their potential by their inability to live or think outside of said three dimensions. Truth is the world and life are multi-dimensional and the true story behind 4.02a.m. is somewhat more complicated and much, much scarier.

You see, as the Devil explained to the cabbie (and he to me) there are not just the different physical worlds in which you and I live; every world also has two spiritual companion worlds and all three of these worlds are intimately and invisibly connected and what happens in one can affect what happens in another. To explain exactly; for each physical world that exists, there is a World Beyond, where most of you will eventually travel, and finally there is a World In-Between. This is the world where the Devil keeps his Special Children. This is the world inhabited by those Souls who are too greedy for the pleasures of the dark side of life in the physical world to let themselves cross over to the World Beyond: Bankers, financiers, corrupt businessmen, politicians, Oligarchs, wife beaters, religious fanatics, bigots, abusers, rapists, buy to let landlords, murderers: evil, sociopathic people, monsters who have profited or pleasured from the Misery And Pain of others.

These Evil Souls gather and wait in the World In-Between and, oh, how they yearn so for the pleasure of causing pain in your world! Like The Devil, they are attracted to misery as a fly to shit. And where there is grief, pain, death, destruction they gather in great numbers and eventually the sheer weight of their wanting tears a hole in the Fabric Of The Universe that separates your world and the one they inhabit and their malignant spirits burst through that tear, at once feeding and growing strong off the misery that they find and making it infinitely worse by virtue of the pervasive miasma of corruption and evil that they leak like Poison in their wake: thus a disease becomes an epidemic, a localised famine spreads country-wide or a regional conflict becomes a major war.

Now the Devil knew that his Special Children would miss the pleasure of causing pain. But he never expected that the strength of their need would tear the universal fabric and allow them to enter the physical world. He was surprised. And delighted. Being a Master of Misery he immediately saw the potential in this strange occurrence. What if he could make this happen not just when there was a "hot spot" of pain, but every day?

The Devil set his mind to things and came up with a plan. He created a Black Magickal Hole in the fabric between your world and the World In-between. A hole that would open up at 4.02am every day, granting access to the living for his Special Children. A perfect way to spread a little despair! He deliberately chose 4.02am as, like scientists and doctors (whom he respects greatly), he knew that at this time the human body is truly at its lowest: at this specific point on the clock, The Devil knew that an injection of despair into the human psyche would have its greatest effect and if his Special Children targeted their efforts on the sick, the vulnerable, the troubled, the down-on-their-luck and those filled with self-doubt, then at worst they could give a person some days of depressive despair or at best they could carry away with them a Soul.

So the next time things aren't going as well for you as they could be and you awake at 4.02am, feeling worthless and panicked, as though life is against you, that all your dreams and ambitions will come to naught, and you sink into a black depression, then remember this little tale. And if you should feel, in the depths of your misery, that some Dark And Brooding Figure is there in the room with you, radiating malice and oozing psychic poison, then it's not your imagination. You're right. It *is* there. Watching you. And it's come to take you away.

But...don't despair. There is an antidote to this - if it happens to you, you can rescue yourself. Don't give in to the siren voice of despair. Remember, instead, that the most boundless and powerful force in the Universe is love and that it has, should you but accept it, woven a web of Gossamer beneath you to catch you should you fall. Remember, too, that you are a unique and capable person (far more than you realise) for in the vastly vast vastness of the Universe a random handful of atoms somehow, against all the odds, came together, travelled across time and space and became you. The odds of that event happening were incalculable, but still it happened and you became you and the incredible odds you defied simply by coming into existence prove that you have a purpose for life and life has a purpose for you.

What would Jesus do?

And so it came to pass, as had been written by the Prophets, that Jesus returned to this world.

One particular day during Jesus' second sojourn on this planet he decided to repeat his Sermon on the Mount speech, you know, the one that goes...

"Blessed are the poor in spirit : for theirs is the kingdom of heaven.

Blessed are they that mourn : for they shall be comforted.

Blessed are the meek : for they shall inherit the earth.

If Blessed are they that hunger and thirst after righteousness..."

...and so on and so on.

Snark aside, it's one of the most beautiful pieces ever

written about love, humility and empathy (all of it nicked from far older, deeper faiths but, hey, that's another story and it makes the words no less important).

Anyway…back to this particular story. So…Jesus having gained some fame on FakeBook (particularly due to the famous and gone viral 'hey look at this freak talking weird stuff about love' meme) a large crowd (a multitude even) soon gathered to hear Jesus give his sermon.

And Jesus stood before the multitude gathered before him and was about to launch into his beautifully crafted plea for love, humility and empathy. But the words stopped in his mouth. For looking at the multitude he did not like what he saw. Half the crowd were tapping away on their iDiotphones, paying no heed to the world around them and forever lost in a universe of one. The rest of the crowd looked hostile or dismissive (sure that this strange man in front of them was about to say something that wasn't on FakeBook and, therefore, to be ridiculed) and the rest had that 'what's in this for me?' look on their faces that Jesus saw so much on this planet and so disliked.

Jesus looked down at his feet. Sighed. Raised his head and said:

'We are gathered here today to talk about love, humility, kindness and empathy...but you know what, sod it, none of these things mean anything to you, you lot are born bad and you're just not worth the trouble. You'll just take my words and twist them, just like you did last time, and use them as an excuse for another two thousand years of racism, homophobia, sexism, bigotry and genocide. So...damn you all, go figure stuff out for yourselves, you bunch of fools, I'm out of here...'

The Nature of Love (Anywhere and Everywhere)

Life…is a random, cacophonous noise full of screaming and shouting and things that glitter and shine but turn out to be not what they seem.

In all that distracting, attention-seeking noise there is only one indisputable constant: Love. For only Love has true and enduring value.

Success and wealth are fabulous, but they are relative and all too often transitory. And at the end of your story on this earth, when the Blind Old Weaver Of Fate is spinning together the final threads of your life, no matter how much success you've gained or how much "stuff" you've bought, they will not hold your hand and mop your brow as your Soul prepares to journey across a Broad, Bright, Blue Sky and your life slips inevitably into The Fog of Forgotten Stories. Only Love will hold you firm. Only Love will gather you up to itself and comfort you, whisper sweet words that calm your Soul and speed it on its final journey to That Which Lies Beyond.

Throughout your life and until The Very End, only love will weave that Shining Web Of Gossamer beneath you, to catch you should you fall.

So don't be distracted by the noise and the bling, by the things that shine so brightly and alluringly, by that which promises much but delivers little. Don't be tempted by regret, hatred and bitterness; they are harsh masters. Don't judge yourself, don't judge others, always walk that mile in another man's shoes. Be kind, be caring; always share and treasure a caress. Seek to leave behind no bad feeling but rather try to add to the Greater Sum of Happiness because everyone, not least yourself, deserves respect, dignity and a chance at life. Above all, remember that to live this life, and leave this world, having loved and having been loved is all that really matters. The rest ain't worth a damn.

I hope you enjoyed my little tales...if you did you can read more tales from Anywhere in my book 'The Dog Who Made The Grim Reaper Cry'. Here's an extract from one of the stories in that book:

God Only Ever Makes One of Each Shoe

<u>Part 1. Doreen's Quest</u>

Once upon a time in the land of Anywhere, in a world long since forgotten, in the fine and prosperous city of Anyplace there lived a dog called Doreen and Doreen was a dachshund, black and tan, smooth-haired, XL, lovely floppy ears, short, stumpy legs and big, chunky dachshund paws. Doreen lived with her family (I say family and not 'owners' because, of course, the idea that any living thing can own another is patently absurd) in a very nice part of Anyplace called Primrose Hill. Doreen had a very lovely, loving family and many friends (doggy, human and other) yet she travelled through her life with an underlying sense of unease and 'not belonging'. You see, Doreen, like many of us, was Different From Others and that Difference always inserted itself as a question mark in all her relationships; always posing the question, even with the closest of her friends, 'do you really, really accept me for what I am?' and creating, for Doreen, what she thought was an Unbridgeable Distance.

As a consequence Doreen, who was a thoughtful and intelligent dog, felt she lived a life that was Semi-Detached from others, and this was a Source Of Sadness to her.

And what exactly, I hear you say, was so Different about Doreen? Well. Doreen could speak. That's right, Doreen was a dachshund who could talk. In truth, talking dogs are not that rare in the land of Anywhere - though rare enough to attract attention and sometimes, from the more ignorant members of the human race, disapproval (another Source Of Sadness to Doreen). As to why Doreen can speak...for that I'm afraid I have no satisfactory answer and if you seek such you'll have to go ask the Faeries, for it is their Mischievous Magick that is at the root of this Unusual Phenomenon.

Anyway, enough of Faeries, let's get back to Doreen. Let's join her on a bright, crisp autumn day. On this day, Doreen awoke in her pleasant home, greeted her family, pestering them for a trip out into the garden and some breakfast and decided to take advantage of the pleasant conditions and do a bit of shopping in nearby Regents Park Road, a part of Primrose Hill filled with Pleasant And Interesting Shops. Now, Doreen didn't actually want to buy anything, as such, for dog's, being far wiser than humans, don't actually need 'stuff' to make them feel 'better' about their lives; for a dog love, companionship, a warm place to sleep and sufficient food to eat are more than enough. Doreen's 'shopping' consisted simply of looking at all the nice, bright, colourful, clever things that the local shopkeepers had for sale and (most of all) sitting down with them for a nice chat over a cup of tea (as well as being able to talk, Doreen was also human-like in her love of a nice cuppa).

So, off to the shops went Doreen. She went in and out of her favourite establishments, examining the wares and chatting about this and that, before coming to her favourite shop all –the shoe shop, for Doreen was very, very fond of shoes.

In she went, greeted the shoemaker and…she fell in love! For there on the shoemaker's counter was a shoe. A single solitary shoe (left foot, size seven). And it was the most beautiful shoe, no - most beautiful thing - she had ever seen. It was a gorgeous stiletto shoe of almost impossible, improbable elegance, covered in rich, red sequins from heel to toe! It shone! It cried out, 'wear me'!

'Wha…wha…what is that!' she stammered to the shoemaker (a kindly old gent with whom she'd passed many a chatty hour).

'It's a beauty isn't it, Doreen…not one I made I'm sorry to say, the level of skill that's gone into that shoe is far beyond me,' replied the shoe maker.

'You know, shoemaker, that is – and I hope you forgive me for saying this given that it's not one of your own creations – the most beautiful shoe I have ever seen! Where did it come? Where's the other one? Where…'

'Woah, woah, Doreen, calm down! You're quite right, it is a truly stunning shoe – no offence taken, by the way – but apart from that I can't tell you more. I have no idea where it came from, where the other half of the pair is or who the maker was…it's a funny thing…the shoe arrived in the post this morning, just on its own, no letter, no paperwork…just a shoe.'

'Can…can I try it on?'

'Of course you may, though I think you may find it a little on the large side even for your big, chunky dachshund paws!'

The shoemaker leaned across his desk, took the shoe in his hand (once again admiring it with a keen professional eye – and a hint of professional envy), walked over to Doreen, bent, and placed the shoe on the floor by her left paw, 'madam…' he said.

Doreen, eyes wide and excited, slowly slid her paw into the shoe and, to both her surprise and that of the shoemaker, it turned out not to be too big…rather it fitted perfectly, seeming almost to mould itself to fit. Doreen, of course, wasn't in the habit of wearing shoes but she knew that had she been she would, at this moment, be thinking something along the lines of 'oh my, I have never worn such a comfortable shoe!'

"Well, look at that, Doreen!' said the shoemaker, excited and amazed, 'that shoe fits you like, well, a glove! I don't know who sent the shoe or who made it but I know why they sent here…so you would find it…here…wait a moment.'

And with that the shoemaker bustled off into the back off his shop and quickly returned with a smart little rucksack, perfectly sized for a dachshund. He knelt down by Doreen, helped her out of the wondrous shoe (she was a bit reluctant to take it off, to be honest), popped it into the rucksack and, smiling, handed it to Doreen and said, 'this is for you, my little dachsie princess, for this shoe was meant to be yours, as surely as the sun rises and sets and the fish swim in the sea.' And Doreen let out a yelp of delight!

Doreen spent another hour or so talking happily with the old shoemaker, made her excuses, slipped her new rucksack (with precious shoe) on to her back and ran all the way home as fast as her short, stumpy dachshund legs and big chunky dachshund paws would allow.

Later that night, after her family had all gone off to sleep, Doreen sat entranced, staring at the shoe. Such a beautiful thing. Where had it come from? Who had made it? Doreen resolved that she had to know the answers to these questions...for some reason, she felt that this was very, very important; a mystery had to be solved and, most of all, she had to find her shoe's partner shoe for every left shoe needs a right shoe, does it not? But where to start? The shoemaker had known nothing of the shoes provenance, apart from it being of exceptional quality. Ah, of course, tomorrow she would pay a visit to Primrose Hill Park to talk to Soho...he was a wise, wise creature and he would know where she should begin her quest – for this was surely a quest, thought Doreen, a quest for what she was not exactly sure but a quest indeed it was.

At this point, reader, I need to both interject and digress, not to interrupt the smooth flow of this tale but to provide you with knowledge about Soho that you will need 'going forward' (as I believe you say in your world).

When Doreen, as a talkative and excitable young puppy, joined her present family, Soho was already there, another dog who had been with Doreen's family for many years. He was a big shaggy, mongrel – a scruffy chap but with a striking coat of many colours, a big heart and a nature that was exceptionally warm and extremely wise. Doreen liked Soho the minute she saw him and they became the firmest of friends, indeed they loved each other deeply and Doreen always considered Soho to be her boyfriend. You can imagine, then, that when Soho passed away three years later, she was devastated. But…only temporarily for Soho's Soul chose not to move on to That Which Lies Beyond but decided to hover between this world and the other. That made him what you in your world would call a ghost. Many Souls choose this course, indeed this world and yours are full of such, they're just not visible (usually) to humans who are incredibly dense in such matters. Some of these souls are good and some are bad. Why the good Souls choose to hover between two worlds, I couldn't tell you except to say that the Soul Knows Its Reasons. The bad souls…well, they choose this way because they are bad, evil to the core. They are the psychopaths, the murderers, politicians, buy to let landlords and members of The Greedy One Percent: they have spent a lifetime inflicting pain, misery and suffering on others and they simply can't give it up, it's an addiction for them so they hang around like an evil miasma, observing and feeding on and stoking the Evil that is present in the world. They are the Devil's Special Children, as much in their deaths as they were in their lives. And the Devil loves them so.

Rest assured, Soho was most definitely a good ghost - how could such a big, loving, soft soul be anything but?

So, the next morning, bright and crisp as the day before, Doreen was up and about early – off she strolled to meet with Soho at their favourite meeting spot in Primrose Hill Park. If you know that particular park (unlikely, granted but, who knows – after all, we've all been to Anywhere some time in our journey, though few of you will remember...) then I can quickly and easily describe to you exactly where they met that day. Picture it. You're standing in the park, with your back to the famous Zoo, facing the hill that rises up in its centre. To the left of the summit of the hill, about three quarters of the way up, is a small stand of trees.

That particular spot, that particular stand of trees, had always been Soho's favourite place to visit (very good sniffing area) and it was exactly where he and Doreen had met every day since he had 'died'.

When Doreen got to that little stand of trees that morning, head still full of thoughts about her mysterious shoe and her exciting quest, Soho was, as always, waiting for her. They greeted each other with delight and spent half an hour saying nothing, just chasing around and around in circles, barking loudly, following up with some boisterous play fighting: this was a strange sight for (human) walkers in the park for all they could see was Doreen, on her own, running around in circles and, seemingly, fighting with herself...they simply didn't know what to make of such a sight for (as I intimated previously), people see so very, very little of the real world in which they live and understand even less.

Exhausted by their play, the two dogs lay down side by side in the crisp air, under that little stand of trees, and Doreen told Soho all about her beautiful shoe, how it made her feel and how she wished to embark on a quest to discover more about the shoe and find the right shoe to match her left her shoe and could he help her?

'Mmm,' said Soho, nodding his big, friendly, shaggy head wisely as was his way, 'I see this is something important to you, Doreen. I feel too, that this is a quest, and one that you should embark upon…I feel there is more to be discovered here than the story of your shoe…'

'Yes, Soho, I agree - but I don't have the first idea where to start or where to go or who to ask about where the shoe came from, who the maker was, where the other one is…and I'm scared by the whole idea because maybe I'll need to leave my home and travel far to find the answers to my questions and I've never left the city of Any place in my life!'

'Doreen, don't think so far ahead, you'll overwhelm yourself with complications and end up doing nothing.

Think of doing just one thing at a time and then the next step will fall into place for you. And you're right, you will have to travel but don't be scared. This is your quest, what you will discover I'm not sure but my heart tells me it is a quest that you must do. Such quests are not unusual in life and we must not let fear stop us doing them...they are there to teach us and help us and those who let fear hold them back may never live the life that they were supposed to live or be the person they were supposed to be. Sometimes, you have to trust fate, you have to have faith and take a step in the dark. Go, Doreen, take your quest, have an adventure, grow, develop...all will be well!'

'But...but...where should I even start!'

'I cannot tell you where you shoe was made or by who, but I can tell you of a wise boy, a portadordeluz, who can answer this question for you...'

'What's a portadorde...thingy...'

'Ah, well, Doreen...there's a tale...are you sitting comfortably? One of the Universal Duties of Faeries, those that gave you the power to speak human speech, my dear, is to rescue any child they come across who is at risk of harm from their parents. Girl children they take away and transform in to faeries, without which practice there would be no new faeries for faeries cannot reproduce. Boy children are a bit more problematic...they cannot become Faeries for all Faeries are female so they are handed over to Trolls who raise the boys as their own. This creates a strange, hybrid creature...a human but with the abilities of Magick and the Insight of a Troll...a portadordeluz. As they grow, these special, wise boys shun human society – with their Troll Insight they understand how gross and cruel it can be – and either stay with their Troll family or become hermits. Their wisdom and advice is much sought out by those few humans that know of these things – those that are poets, visionaries, writers or considered by others to be mad. I happen to know of one such boy and where you can find him, still young, still living with trolls. I feel for sure that he will know where your shoe came from. Do you wish to know how to find him, Doreen? Do you wish to begin your quest!?'

'Yes! Yes!'

'Good! Now, Doreen, roll over here and place your nose against mine...that's it...good...now match your breathing with mine, close your eyes and let your mind drift...'

Which is exactly what she did and as she did so a picture went from Soho's mind to hers, not so much a picture, though, more a map but not as you would recognise a map with roads and contour lines and gradients and suchlike, for it was a doggy map made up smells and sights and Doreen smelt a fish, a big fish, a fox and a crow and she saw a broad river, a dense forest and wide open, grassy plain. And this she knew was the route that would take her to the wise boy, the portadordeluz.

That very night, Doreen informed her family of her intention to go on her quest, she even showed them her shoe, and being easy-going and generous people they, too, agreed that Doreen should undertake her trip and gave her their blessings.

The next morning Doreen woke with a thrill of excitement, tinged with a hint of fear, and thought to herself 'right, well, no point hanging about…off I go!'....

She took the rucksack given to her by the kindly old shoemaker and into it she packed her wonderful shoe and eight pork pies (pork pies being Doreen's favourite food), eight pies being chosen on the basis that she judged, from the map Soho had planted in her mind, that her journey would take two days, four pies a day – should be enough!

And off she went....

What happens next? Buy the book and find out!

Printed in Great Britain
by Amazon

63502007R00068